# FRAGMENTS OF MY HEART

BY

MOUMITA BASU

ISBN 978-93-5438-436-3

Published in India 2020 by Pencil

*A brand of*

One Point Six Technologies Pvt. Ltd.
123, Building J2, Shram Seva Premises,
Wadala Truck Terminal, Wadala (E)
Mumbai 400037, Maharashtra, INDIA
**E** connect@thepencilapp.com
**W** www.thepencilapp.com

# Author biography

Moumita Basu grew up in West Bengal, India where she spent twenty blissful years with her family before moving to Bangalore in order to pursue her career as a full time software engineer. She loves reading quotes, poetries and romance novels which inspires her to write everyday. Her debut poetry book 'Fragments Of My Heart' is a collection of her life experiences while growing up. It talks about Love, Friendship, Heartbreak, Relationship and other aspects of life.

You can find her on Instagram - @moumitabasuwrites

# Contents

# Her

Caged Bird
An extremely hot evening without any rain.
Yet there she was; standing under the sun.
Enjoying how the sun caressed her skin.
She knew it would last only for a while
so why not make the most of it?

So she ran, jumped, skidded but as soon as
the sun went down, reality set in.
She is an eagle soaring high in the sky
when she is outside but once inside
she is just 'A caged bird'.


Bare Soul
Come,
seek my soul
if you dare.

Like that empty

bottle of liquor
& wine glass,

it is lying bare.


Warrior In Disguise

Neither a princess waiting for Prince Charming,

nor a damsel in distress who needed saving.

There was pain and anger in her eyes  which
she masked beautifully with her angelic smile;

Only few people could recognise

that she was a 'Warrior In Disguise'.


Her World
She was looking for

an escape everyday;

To her this world

always felt unreal

because she always

dreamt of living

in a world which
was way beyond
anyone's imagination
and much bigger than

reality.


The Dreamer

I am a dreamer.

I grew up reading fairytales, mysteries, short stories and novels.

My fingers would always be restless just like my mind,

devouring page after page

and once the story comes to an end,

it would leave me wanting for more...for that essence
something which I cannot describe or explain.
Love for the Moon

I love the moon because she's scarred
yet looks so sacred,
she keeps her word,
rising every evening after sunset,
she spreads light wherever there's darkness.

In the night sky, so vast,
her pale face is a contrast
and whenever I look at up to see her,
she reminds me of my past

# The Magic Portal

It was a cold winter morning,

my teeth were chattering.

I checked the calendar date,

21st December it read.


I thought of writing something

but my mind wasn't working.

So I opened Instagram to check
likes and comments on my latest poem.

Alas! Someone has written "Crappy"

and that definitely made me sappy.


I wanted to disappear from this world

where everyone was rude and judgemental,

when I saw a ray of light streaking through

the keyhole....
wait was it 'The Magic Portal'?


Curious, I opened the door and found myself

walking into a vast meadow where everything

looked green and blue!

Leaves rustling, butterflies perched on flowers,
birds flying...

Indeed a fascinating view!


Wondering what else was in store

I decided to explore;

and saw people of different age groups

either reading books,

writing in notebooks,

drawing in sketchbooks,

or singing and dancing

by the brook.


There wasn't any sign of smartphones,vehicles
or buildings towering over you.

Just genuine smile and joy in people's eyes

and I realized dreams do come true!

Won't it be amazing to live here...

in this magical world where nobody would

judge you for being 'YOU'?

# Not A Toy

She is looking for someone
who would make her a priority,

not make her feel like a casual fling,

someone consistent in his actions,
talk to her frequently and appreciate
what she does not because it's a duty
but because he wants to do it,

someone who understands her emotions
without having her to explain him

or complain every single time
"you don't understand me",

someone who makes her believe that
true love exists and it's safe to trust
instead of saying "trust no one" and
crush her hopes and beliefs,

someone who shows interest in her
because he actually finds her interesting,

not to play with her emotions, boost his ego
and suck out all her positive energy.

No darling, she isn't looking for a man who
would love her practically.

Remember, she is already dealing with a lot -
balancing health, career, family, friends and
at the same time going through anxiety,

a broken heart and a past which is messed up.

If you don't wanna make her happy,
please don't pretend to like her for
your own needs.
She's not a toy you can play with.

# True Friend

Someone with whom you can blend

Someone who won't offend

Someone who is there to defend

Someone on whom you can depend

Someone who will never pretend

Someone with whom you love to
spend your weekend

Someone who will always be closer
to you than your girlfriend or boyfriend

Someone without whom you might
feel the world will come to an end.

That someone is no one but
'Your true friend'.

# The Perfect Daughter

Maybe she is still a kid at heart

Maybe she is not too smart

Sometimes she makes mistakes
without even knowing

For which she hopes she will be
forgiven, just saying.


She acts like she doesn't care
when she gets a scolding

So that she doesn't break down
because her heart is aching

It was never her intention to be a burden

She just needed those depressing days
to brighten.


When she spent long nights crying

She wanted her parents to know that
she has not given up but still trying

It is her promise she won't be a dissapointment

When everybody hated her all she needed
was a compliment


Too many questions without any answer

I am sorry but she is not
'The perfect daughter'.

# My Best Friend

Like the unexpected wind that blows across the sea

She walked into my life with a glee.

Two strangers who just crossed paths, I agree

But I was the lock, she was my key.


It started with the story of 'Avatar'

I still can't believe our friendship would go this far

Sometimes I wish I could hold all our memories in a jar

Coz they are so precious to me, like that morning star.


People created misunderstandings thinking they are smart

Trying every means to weaken our heart

But that never worked out coz sweetheart

Our friendship is too strong to break us apart.


Eight years - Yes, that long we have been best - friends

I promise one day we will get a job and live together in the highlands

Now that would be fun, don't you think 'My best friend'?

Untill our last breath, hey, but our friendship will never end.

# Mother Nature

## I

Everybody is always in a rush

Why don't you stop for a moment
and hush?

Just sit down and be still

Close your eyes, don't frown

Can you feel the thrill?

Of the wind blowing

birds chirping

river flowing

and the moon glowing?

The best possible gift given to
mankind is nature

'Do spend some time with her' -
says our creator.

## II

As dawn breaks, that ray of hope

Slowly peeking up in the sky.

With burning rage, intimidating

Every soul that meets the eye.
Eyes closed, rustling of leaves
As the wind gently caressed.
A relief from the burning coal
Approaching from northwest.
With dusk setting in,the birds
Fearless, flying towards home.
Just like the red chunk of ball
Touching the sea and its gloam.
I want to click pictures and
Capture these moments.
In the end we are left with
Memories made up of fragments.

# I Loved, He Left

"And all along our love was just an  illusion where you and I
were imaginery."

I

I am that miserable girl

who fell in love with a jerk.

who never gave a damn

about my feelings yet I

cared about him so much.

I was sure he'd notice me

one day....after all I loved

him so deeply but he didn't.

He hung out with other

girls which hurt me so bad.

And I kept thinking why

is it that he never loves

me back?

Is this how one sided love

feels like?

II

And after years
when I saw you
walking down the street
with a beautiful girl
Did my heart cry?

Down the alley,
across the street,
when you were smiling
at her witty jokes,
I should have turned away
but why didn't I?

Our eyes met
as we crossed paths.
You said,
"Hello. Have a nice evening"
leaving me again this time
holding hands with
the love of your life
and bidding me

a goodbye.

Inspite of watching you leave,
I smiled.
Yet,
after reaching home
why did my heart,
feel so heavy
the whole night?

# I Loved, He Betrayed

"Why did I give him my heart when all he did was rip it apart?"

I


"I have major trust issues", she said, her heart beating fast.

"Don't worry, tell me everything sweetheart. I'll make sure to heal all your scars", he said, knowing very well how much it hurts when someone breaks your trust.

But could he really learn how to trust again and heal her scar?

Or would he just wake up in the morning, forget the entire conversation and just leave her?


II


The red flags told me to walk away from him.

but I didn't.

What did I expect?

For him to change?

For this time to be different?


III


I didn't blink.

Just stared.

I didn't move.

Just wished

I wasn't there.

The bouquet of

flowers fell down

on the floor;

At once,

I clasped the handle

of the door,

pulling it down like

never before

hoping I was quick

enough to walk out

without a permanent

eyesore.

IV

I cried that night,

after we broke up.

The next day I saw you

standing outside  with a girl;

How will I deal  with this pain,

this hurt?

After all,  you gave me

'The lover's  curse' .

# I Loved, He Played

"No matter where I go, some memories will never leave me
alone"

The Playboy

You kissed my forehead

filling my heart with joy.

And then you started

unbuttoning my shirt

planting kisses on my

body as if I were a toy.

Oh how I wish I knew

from the beginning that

you were a playboy!

Not My Knight

I thought you were my saviour that night,

when you listened to my plight.

So I looked at you in delight

and mistook your insight

thinking, everything will be alright.

Oh boy so wrong was I!

Because not only did you lie

but you played both my heart and mind,

surrounded my life with darkness

instead of light,

sucked all of my energy

like a blood sucking parasite

and took my soul like a devil in disguise.

That's when I realised

that I was never your fallen angel and

neither were you my knight.


Devil In Disguise


She made a deal with a guy

who turned out to be

THE DEVIL IN DISGUISE

He was the definition of

MR. PERFECT outside

so when he offered her

to enter his den,

she didn't deny.
But as soon as she stepped inside,
the sweet guy put his mask aside
revealing his true face which almost
brought tears to her eyes.
How could she possibly sleep at night
knowing very well that the devil can
force himself on her anytime while
she was sleeping;
They were lying alongside!

# I Loved, He Stayed

"He gave me a million reasons to choose him everyday and so I did"

I

My mind was at ease,

heart, in peace.

To be in love with someone
who loves you back,

is this is how true love feels?

II

I don't wanna say goodbye

I don't wanna cry

I don't wanna miss you tonight

I just want to hold you tight

and say, "Baby it's alright.

I know I'm not a perfect guy

but for you I wanna try"

III

It was one of those winter evenings when they decided to take a
walk down the road less travelled by.
The evening sky was already pink with a hint of purple and
orange; not to mention the humongous trees
whose names they didn't know but that only added to the
evening's charm.

"If money, work, family wasn't an issue would you choose to be
here always?", he asked her.

"I would give anything to choose this life,"

she said, to which he held her hand, pulled her close and planted
a kiss on her forehead.

"It's rare to find love this pure," he thought

That night, after making love for a long time, she fell asleep first.
He could sense her emotions and thought why not?

It was barely dawn.He got up and went outside for a walk.

Staring at both of their phones one last time, he just threw them
away as they went rattling down the rocky terrain
breaking into God knows how many pieces.

"Countryside it is then", he said, as the wind swept his hair,
highly impressed leaving him behind with a smile.

# Living And Dead

Every girl's fantasy, every boy's dream.

He was popular, she was a nerd.

He played football, she read books.

The first time they met

her heart skipped a beat, his didn't.


His tears, her weakness.

His smile, her strength.

His anger, her fear.

The first time they talked

she looked deep into his eyes, he didn't.


Her smartness, his envy.

Her cuteness, his annoyance.

Her crush, his enemy.

The day she proposed

he blocked her from facebook,
she couldn't block him from her heart.

True Love Never Dies

So today I'll sit down on the chair

Or maybe lie down on my bed

Replaying a memory in my head

For which my heart might bleed but I don't care.


With eyes closed and a small lingering smile

I will relive that moment

Again and again

Until we are just a mile.


I know as time flies

Memories fade, people move on and bid goodbyes

But sometimes our heart still cries

Because 'True love never dies'.

# The Seasons

### Autumn

### I

He walked into her life like a hurricane,
only to turn her world upside down and
imprint her soul with scars so deep that
she could never fall in love again.

### II

And when you pulled me closer to your lips,
I realized we've fallen down deep on a very
lazy Sunday morning just like two autumn
leaves.

### Summer

### I

She couldn't resist him,

her eyes closed under
the magical spell of the
dandelion flowers, it was
almost a fantasy to see

him again on a summer
day dream.

II

Summer brought back
memories of her unkept
promises which she
swore to keep one day
but like him, forgot about
them anyway.

Spring

She knew their relationship was doomed

from the beginning and he would leave someday

yet she hoped that he would stay

just like the spring flowers bloomed

every year until May

and she would love him for another day.

Winter

I

I don't know what hurts me more.
Last summer when you wanted
me to love you and I didn't or
this winter when you decided to
move on but I couldn't.


II


I compose wistful poetries every
winter because each day reminds
me of my shattered heart when
you left me for another.

# The Last Few Days

I

Walking past a cavern

she took a turn -

A soul scarred with spurn,

holding a lantern.

With faded yearn,

Disconcern,

she promised to return -

The day her lamp would burn.

II

"I'm sorry", he said.

She was standing like a statue,
staring at his retreating figure
as he left.

Dark clouds, grey sky
It was a rainy day.

"I'm sorry", she said.

He was sitting beside the window sill,
holding her hands when she took her
last breath.

Dark clouds, grey sky
Yet another rainy day.

III

When the cold wind blew

across the wide blue sea,

there was a little girl

slowly making her way

towards the beach.

She left behind footprints

until a wave came crashing
down at her feet and swept
away all her memories.

IV

When the cold wind blew

right through his chest,

he came crumbling down

on the floor with a zest

Under the wintry air and sky

he lay,

observing people passing by

every single day.
The winter wind howled
and he called for help every night
making her heart ache
to see such a sight
One day when a tiny streak of sunlight
passed through her window sill
she knew it was summer once again
and woke up with a thrill
But I guess it was too late
because before she opened her eyes
he had already withered faraway
leaving each to their own fate.

# Living Without Them

You meet a stranger

With him, you feel so connected

That he becomes your family member.

That's when your obsession start

He controls your mind, body and soul

Until you burst.

Sometimes people enter your life

To teach you how to live without someone

So when they leave make it worthwhile

By not cutting yourself with a knife.

# Be Aware Of Players

First they'll charm you

Then say, "I love you"

Followed by

controlling you,

possessing you

owning you

and this game

will continue

until they

break you.

# Cherish What You Have

While chasing after something we 'Don't have'

At times we forget about things we

'Do have'

So today be thankful for the

People who are a part of your life

Things you possess

Beating heart which has kept you alive

Memories you have come across.

Cherish them.

# Living Life To The Fullest

So what if you lost someone in the past?

Trust me, it was never meant to last.

Today when you sit back and think about it

Cry all you want but never quit.

Your past does not define your present

So be brave, take risks without being determent.

Tomorrow is a mystery so stop worrying about your future

Live your present, enjoy life coz it's an adventure.

Today you might face an obstacle

Tomorrow there may be a miracle.

Live your life today to the fullest

If you want your tomorrow to be  - 'The greatest'.

# Things You Must Never Do

Never settle for less

Never beg to be loved

Never give up

Never let someone treat you as an option

Never ignore your gut instinct

Never be too available for anyone

Never trust players

Never rush while taking a decision

Never stop chasing your dreams

Never love anyone more than yourself

# Life And Love

### I

Life is not about 'Just Dreaming'

Life is about working hard,
staying dedicated to your goals
so that one day you can proudly
say - 'Yes I turned my dream into reality'

### II

Love is not pretending, manipulating, pursuading or forcing
your better half to love you back

Love is kind, not selfish

Love is free, not something you beg for

Love is not just about romance and getting physical

True love doesn't hurt or make a person stop believing in the L
word forever

Love is about trust, care, respect and admiration for your partner
lifelong.

# Just Breathe

I have always imagined this scenario in my head
where one day we would wake up in the morning,
just to feel the fresh air against our skin,
admire the beautiful sky, the vastness of the sea
and our surrounding.
A day when we would value life and understand
it's meaning instead of cursing and grieving.
We won't worry about time slipping, or if
something's missing...
That day we would just be in the moment breathing.

# The Other End Of The Line

Soulful eye

Enchanting smile

Hearts that cry;

Sitting on a handrail

side by side,

on a Friday night,

were two strangers

silently observing city lights,

people passing by,

jostling crowd,

honking cars,

defeating traffic lights,

just to reach the

other end of the line

on time.

# Mental Health

No matter what you do or say, some people are just born to give
you stress

When they get mad you're expected to be calm and understand
but when it comes to you,
they tell you to grow up or they're gonna start a nuclear war.

They are self centred and egomaniacs who neither gives
compliment nor knows how to take them

They will hurt your sentiment, get annoyed for no reason and
then act like you hurt them

They think they're always right and you're wrong in the end

It's pointless wasting your time and energy on such people as they
are gonna treat you like crap anyway

Only the people who care about you...you should care for them.

# The Writer

People often ask me why do I always write about love,
relationships, heartbreaks and feelings?

Am I in love? No

Am I heartbroken? No

Am I in a relationship? No

"So then why do you insist that true love exists?" someone asked
me.


People experience heartbreak every day, get cheated by someone,
get hurt by being in a toxic relationship...
the list is endless and when it's too much to take in, they just
lock their heart, throw away the key and stop
feeling. But tell me one thing - bottling up your emotions will
save you from getting hurt but without feelings,
does that even you a human being?


So that's the reason I write about love, relationships, heartbreaks
and feelings..for people to embrace their
emotions, be it happy or sad because that's what makes us more
human and less of a machine, to be kind
and have an open heart because believe me when I say this - you
won't realize when love will walk into
your life unknowingly leaving you surprised at destiny.

www.ingramcontent.com/pod-product-compliance
Lightning Source LLC
LaVergne TN
LVHW050426160726
843469LV00041B/1246